AF429641

Chaotic Roots

Choosing Chaos, Volume 0.5

MJ Hutto

Published by MJ Hutto, 2023.

This is a work of fiction. Similarities to real people, places, or events are entirely coincidental.

CHAOTIC ROOTS

First edition. October 14, 2023.

Copyright © 2023 MJ Hutto.

ISBN: 979-8230237464

Written by MJ Hutto.

Chaotic

Roots

By: MJ Hutto
A KableVerse Adventure Prequel

<u>**Witch, Spy, Adventurer Extraordinaire**</u>
<u>**Cheap Thrill**</u>
<u>**The Choices We Make**</u>
<u>**Devil, Demon, Guardian**</u>
<u>**Endings, Beginnings, Forever**</u>
<u>**Fairy Tales Or Faery Tails**</u>

Fynbar & Ekaterina

One constant in Kable's life is her grandparents. Their love and devotion to each other and to her has shown her that love exists in a world seemingly determined to crush gentle souls. Too bad for the world she's learning how to be fierce.

The first five stories give you a look at who they were before and the last is a peek into who they were when Kable knew them.

I hope you'll enjoy this Novella where you get to meet the young souls of the people that shaped her into the fierce, beautiful soul she is.

LOVE YA,

MJ

Witch, Spy, Adventurer Extraordinaire

Fynbar Prequel

EXPLOSIONS LIGHT UP the dark midnight sky, ruining my night vision and giving away my position. I didn't mean for there to be that much *oomph* behind that potion. Maybe the dragon's breath I used had been a little over the top. The Drake had donated it willingly, if not happily. I tap my lip. Maybe that's why. But, enough contemplation, the guards are about to be upon me.

"Drake! Where are you, you useless lizard?" I yell into the night, and suddenly a dark shadow crosses the sky. *The Drake is my familiar and one of the largest dragons ever to grace this Earth. I am Fynbar Farrel—Witch, spy, adventurer extraordinaire. Pleased to meet you.*

The Drake lets out a great, resounding, bowel-loosening roar, which he ends with a small spurt of fire for punctuation. The group of twenty guards that is nearly upon me stops short. My partner in crime swoops down into the clearing, snatching me up with his talons. The guards yell, thrusting their swords and staves into the air but not coming close to hurting either of us.

Well, until one of them gets smart and pulls out his bow. The first arrow whizzes by my ear, and I'm worried it might've taken one of my freckles with it. The second catches some of my hair, pulling it out by the roots; happily, it misses the rest of me and my ride, but I can see the red strands entangled as it sails away. I mutter a quick Spellword to ignite the hairs—can't have someone getting ahold of something like that. They could use it to find me, and I'm not really in a position for company.

As we climb higher, the arrows fall short. Suddenly, I'm freefalling through the air, but Drake swoops underneath and catches me on his back. The landing is rough and painful, but I'm astride and holding on.

"Woo!!!" I yell as the wind whips my hair around and throw my arms up joyously. I'm not afraid of falling; Drake and I have done this thousands of times—the flying, not the running from castle guards. This high, the air is cold and thin, and my clothes aren't the warmest. I pat the side of his neck, and he turns towards our current domicile. I lean down and let his massive neck and body shield me from some of the more brutal wind.

He lands in a field with a running, jolting stop. If you've ever ridden a horse, it's sort of like that, except there's no saddle or harness, and he does whatever the hell he wants.

He turns his large dark head around to stare at me with a luminous red eye. "You nearly got us killed, you moron. What were you doing so close to all those guards? You were supposed to sneak out and meet me. What did you do?"

I scowl up at him with a raised fist. "Me? You weren't where you were supposed to be." But he's right. I didn't do what I was supposed to. "There was this girl."

He rolls his eyes and strolls toward the cave we use as our hideout. It's behind a waterfall that feeds into a lake, very cliché. "There's always a girl, Fyn. Your junk is going to get you killed. And!" he says, puffing out smoke and glowering. "More importantly, it's going to get me killed. I am a majestic and beautiful creature. STOP trying to end that for me!"

I mimic him, shaking my head back and forth as I follow him into the cave. There's a small ledge that lets me in without soaking me through. I cup my hands, drink some of the fresh, cold water, and wash my face before turning toward my angry friend. "You're right. I'll be more careful," his head swivels around, and if you've never seen a giant dragon brow raised in supercilious fashion, you haven't lived. "Honest, I'll try!"

"Did you at least get it?" he asks in exasperation, throwing his head back and rolling over onto his side. "Come get his arrow out of my tail."

"They hit you?" I exclaim and sprint over to him. "Where? Why didn't you say something? Of course, I got it."

An arrow sticks halfway into the meatier portion of his long tail. "I just said something. It's only the one," he utters gruffly. "It was heading straight for your stupid face, and I know how much you value your supposed gorgeousness. I couldn't let that get marred now, could I?"

I bray out a laugh and put my hand at the base of the arrow. Magic doesn't penetrate dragons very well, it's one reason they are usually killed with physical weapons instead of magical ones, so I can't do much more than pull it out. I start counting, and before I reach three jerk it out swiftly. His answering roar shakes the walls, and dirt showers down over us.

I wash the wound with fresh water. His elevated body temperature and natural healing will take care of the rest. Task completed, I sit beside the fire he breathes into existence and pull out some dried fruit to eat.

"Where is it?" he asks quietly.

I grin and pull out a ruby necklace. It's set in a dark filagree with a long, peculiarly cold chain. It sparkles and glows and dances in the firelight.

"I pulled it off the neck of the Queen," I tell him smugly.

"Is that why the guards were after you?"

I laugh with satisfaction. "No, she was too busy enjoying the glorious kiss I bestowed upon her. The guards were because the *King* did not appreciate the kiss or me in their bed."

He laughs uproariously, his head thrown back. "Of course! At least it was only your lips this time!"

Cheap Thrill

Fynbar & Ekaterina

I CARESSED THE PALM of the fiery devil in front of me. His hands were callused and rough from whatever work he performed. His eyes were grey like storm clouds, and his hair was red copper on fire. He glanced down at his hand in mine and grinned boyishly.

"What say you, Ms. Cooper, will I live a long life?"

I lifted a brow in amusement. "Not if you keep interrupting me, Mr. Farrel. As I've told you once already."

He drew in a breath and nodded as he looked around my room. We were in my outer sitting area, where I performed palm readings. He'd been by the day before but hadn't come inside. He'd watched me dance but hadn't come for a reading until today.

"Your lifeline has many branches. It extends well past your palms. I think you will live to a very old age," I tell him as I smooth my thumb over the lifeline on his palm again. It doesn't really mean anything like that, but people always wanted to hear it. It did look like he had excellent health, a positive attitude, and was enthusiastic, courageous, and full of vitality. It really meant the same thing.

"Your love line is jagged initially but smooths out about halfway. You've loved many for a short time, but someday you will love *one* for *eternity*."

His eyes met mine, and a warm sizzle of electricity began where our hands met. It traveled down my heart cord to my core and spread to every nerve ending. His breath caught, the world did a counter spin, my face heated, his lips parted, and my betrothed walked into the room.

I glanced uncertainly up at both Mr. Farrel and Domino. The latter glared at us with icy blue eyes. His blond hair was tied back in a tail, showing off his handsome features. They were considerably less attractive at the moment, related to his angry scowl.

"You are supposed to be on stage. What are you doing here?"

Domino was my betrothed, an old tradition my family still subscribed to. Our families were to be combined through the two of us when we married in two months' time. We were fated to change the course of history.

A combination from the families Cooper and Vitoli two will result in a world that is new.

I am not convinced it means what they all seem to think. Domino seems convinced but unhappy. He was less interested even than I; his kisses half-hearted, his interest feigned, his caresses cool. It felt as if I was a dreaded chore he must contend with. I was not happy; he was not happy. We were moving through an unfortunate task, and I worried it would remain so. The cards told me it was true. I looked into the laughing grey eyes of the man across from me and narrowed my own. He was trouble. I patted his hand and stood to meet my future husband.

"You didn't finish my reading."

Domino's hand on my shoulder drew my gaze between the two of them. I nodded to Domino to assure him I understood my obligations and turned back to the paying customer.

"I must be on stage in a few minutes. I will return in thirty minutes time if you wish a longer reading. Or you can go to another tent, and one of the others will gladly read for you. They have fewer obligations," I told him.

His eyes moved from my face to the towering man behind me. I was not a large woman at barely five feet, but Domino was a near giant at six foot nine. His thigh was the size of my waist. He was rumored to have the blood of giants in his family tree.

"I think I'd like to wait if it's all the same. I'd rather have the finished read from you if I may."

Domino grunted and pulled me from the room. I followed behind him, pulling my top off, grabbing my costume on the way by, and pulling it over my head. I skidded to a stop to pull off my shoes, and Domino nearly yanked my arm off.

"What are you doing?" I hissed at him. "He's willing to pay a lot for a reading."

"He doesn't want a reading. He wants a taste of a Cooper."

I laughed at him. "What do you care? Last week, you were ready to sell tickets."

He threw his hands up in the air and turned to glower at me. "I was not. It was a joke."

"Domino, I dance in front of a room full of men and women several times a day. Why does this one bother you?" I asked as I pulled on my veil and scarves.

"He is not like the others."

I laughed. "He is like all the others, my friend. Are you jealous? Do you wish he looked at you as he is looking at me?"

He grabbed my arm roughly and looked around. "Do not say such things so loudly. They are always listening 'Rina."

I touched his face. "You deserve to be happy, Dom. Not this farce of a life. The prophecy doesn't mean what they all think. My darling friend, we can change the world together and not *be* together. It does not have to be a life sentence for either of us."

He leaned back against the wall beside the door to the dance hall. His face was a mask of petulance and despair. "Ah, 'Rina, I wish it was as you say. I am tired of pretending," he said, then grinned. "And I am a little jealous your copper-haired friend has eyes only for you. What can I expect when you are such a shining jewel? Alas, the raven-haired, blue-eyed beauty with luscious..." he made a motion in front of his chest, and I swatted him.

"Funny. Very funny," I said, pulling the skirt down. "Your day will come. We aren't getting married. I won't tie you to me for a stupid prophecy that isn't even true. We'll find a way out of this."

He sighed heavily and helped me adjust my scarves. I held out my arms for inspection. He flounced the skirt a few times and pronounced me done with a wave.

"Your lips to Universe's ears," he said, kissing his fingers and tossing it to the sky.

I stood on tiptoe, kissed his cheek, and grinned. "I always get my way, darling. It will be done."

I FINISHED MY DANCES and picked up a drink at the bar. I was met there by Mr. Farrel. His eyes shone, and he lifted the glass to me in salute. I returned the gesture and shook my head.

Trouble, indeed.

My sister Nataylia was next, and she brought baby Bohdan over to me while she did her part for the family. She'd been joined to the Angeloff family, but they'd remained here with us.

"Hello, sweet boy," I said, leaving the drink off and taking him out of the hall. I made sure she saw us leaving and pointed towards my tent. She could come to get him after she finished. She was serving tonight, too. I only had my dances and then readings to do. He would be fine with me.

He gurgled up at me with a sweet smile. He smelled like baby powder and sunshine. The air was chilly, so I snuggled baby Bohdan close and hurried to my tent. He laid his head on my shoulder and burbled. I heard footsteps behind me and turned to smile up at the troublesome red-haired Irishman. He wasn't tall like Dom, but he was still head and shoulders above me, with broad shoulders and a chest that strained the buttons on his fine linen shirt. His eyebrows were raised when he saw the baby.

"You have a babe?"

I kissed Bohdan's downy, soft hair. "He's my nephew. My sister is dancing now, so I'm watching him for her. Come in. I'll finish your reading."

He followed me inside. I sat down at the table, and he followed suit.

"I'm not really here for a palm reading," he said.

"Oh," I replied and pulled out my tarot deck. I'd laid out the cards before he answered.

"Not a tarot read either. I'm looking for a guide."

I glanced up at him, smoothing my hand over Bohdan's back in circles. He was almost asleep, so I kept my voice soft and evenly soothing.

"What sort of guide, Mr. Farrel? I am not a guide. I am a dancer and a fortune teller."

He looked around the room, face no longer soft. His features were bland but held mild curiosity.

"What do you know of the Ural Mountains?"

My eyes narrowed in thought. "Some. It's a dangerous place. Especially for one like you."

"Like me?"

I laughed softly, continuing to soothe the sleeping babe. "Yes, like you. You do not blend, nor do you fade into the background. You are like an exotic bird, not easily ignored or forgotten."

His straight, white teeth gleamed behind smiling lips. His smile was infectious in its purity and joy. "I do believe that is the first time I've been called too pretty. I find I quite like it."

His grey eyes sparkled, and I felt an answering smile spreading across my face. "What do you need in the mountains? And what are you offering for my help? I don't come cheap, sir."

His face remained happy, but the smile drifted away. He cocked his head to the side before the smile returned with a snap of his fingers. He reached into a pocket hidden on his pants leg and pulled out a velvet pouch. He held it in his hands while he talked.

"I am in search of the stone giants."

I frowned, confused. "Why? How do you know of the brothers?"

"Does it matter why?"

I thought about the answer. "I'm afraid it does. I believe in the magic of the place. If you mean to deface or harm it. I'll not be a part of that."

"I've no plans to deface or harm a thing. I'm looking for a book. I've been told it might be there."

My brows furrowed.

"I'm confused. A book? In the mountains with the stone giants? How did it supposedly get there? How is it still there and whole?"

He smiled softly when the baby nuzzled my neck. "It's magic, love."

My brows lowered further, and a sound of exasperation eased out. "Is it now? I suppose you know a lot about that, do you? You're awfully tall for a leprechaun."

He laughed abruptly, making the baby startle. When I'd quieted him again, Mr. Farrel had an appropriately contrite look on his face.

"My apologies. I'd not wake the babe for anything. You surprised me with your candor, madame. I have no leprechaun blood; my line runs a bit more towards Faery."

"Mmm," I grunted. That explained why I had such a hard time telling him to get lost and keeping my eyes off his beautiful features. *TROUBLE.* "I see. Mr. Farrel..."

"Please, call me Fyn or Fynbar."

"We'll see. What precisely do you need from me? And I ask again, what are you offering?"

"I need a guide through the mountains to the stone giants. I was told you are the best."

"That's true enough. And your offer?"

He pulled up the velvet pouch and dumped the contents into his hand. The candles in the room caught the gemstone, making it sparkle deeply. It was beautiful and called out to me. The ruby was red fire shimmering in the candlelight. He held it out to me, and I touched it gently with my fingertips.

A sudden tingling warmth surged from my fingertips, down my arm, and to...well, other places. I drew in a breath and made myself take my hand away. My heart raced, and when I looked up into those grey eyes, I saw that he, too, was breathing fast. I snatched the necklace from him.

"Done."

The Choices We Make

Fynbar & Ekaterina

"Madame, are you wearing pants?"

"Are you going to have a problem with everything I do? It's will take twice as long if I must explain myself to you every time I do something."

I quirked a brow at the raven-haired spitfire standing across from me. She barely came up to my shoulder but radiated authority. I held my hands up in surrender.

"I was merely making conversation. Also, I was going to say it was a good idea. I've heard the mountains are very cold right now. I'd thought to loan you some if you didn't have any."

She snorted, and I grinned despite myself.

"Then you're a fool. Nothing you have that fits you would come close to fitting me. And I'll be thanking you not to give me another woman's clothes that you've kept as a remembrance, Fynbar Farrel."

She was all fire and challenge. I'd never met anyone like her. And she knew magic. Not that fake, sleight of hand or scheming mess...real magic, like mine. She glared back over her shoulder at me from where watched her.

"Are you staring at my backside?" she asked suspiciously.

I inhaled to answer when her ogre of a fiancée came over. To be fair, he was ogre in size only. He wasn't ugly at all. He had kind of a nice face that I wanted very much to punch, just because it was nice. Instead, I smiled at them both.

"I'll get the horses ready," I told them, walking into the distance to put my pack on the horse her family has generously rented to me. He, at least, looked sturdy. I twisted the ring on my left pinky around halfway and said the Word in my head to engage it. It would allow me to hear them without appearing to do so.

Don't look at me like that. If they are planning to kill me, I need to know. She's rather beautiful, but those are the ones that sneak up on you. Now, let me listen.

"I see the way he looks at you 'Rina," from the fiancée.

"You don't actually care, Dom. You aren't jealous of me. Maybe I can find something to help us out of this farce created by false prophesies. He's looking for a book there. Maybe it could help us, too."

"You will steal from him? And bring that luck down upon us, too?"

She scoffed. "No, I thought to borrow it...or maybe he would help me."

He laughed at her sardonically. "And what will that cost you?"

"What does it matter if we are no longer stuck in this trap," she retorted sharply.

They paused, and I realized I had been still too long. I moved around the horse, checking the saddle and stirrups. They began talking again.

"I care about you 'Rina. I do not wish you to sell your soul so that I may love who I choose."

"And what of me?" she asked hotly. "Who I want, what I want doesn't matter? Why? Because I do not have one of those tiny worms hanging between my legs?"

I almost laughed aloud at that but managed to catch myself before it slipped out. I patted the horse and turned to check the other.

"I did not mean that at all," he grumbled at her. "But if you continue to talk like that, none will have you. They don't look at you now because you dance like what you have is yours solely to give."

She laughed. "It is, I have, and I will continue to do so. I dare another to say differently. And they do not look at me because they think I am yours."

"Yes, as your fiancée, they have come to me. Laughed at me."

She laughed. "And how many times has your cave been plundered, Dom? Your jewels explored by strong hands? Your worm devoured? No one came to me, not once."

He choked out a strangled sound, and I began to understand. He has NO interest in the fair Ekaterina. His interests fell somewhere with broader shoulders and fewer curves. I happened to know an army general who had similar tastes. They could, perhaps, fulfill prophesies together, leaving the fiery Ekaterina to blaze her own paths.

"Someone will hear you," he hissed. "They will ostracize me. Kick me from the family."

She scoffed again. "They will do no such thing. You will be a strong leader, and they want you in our family. They want us to bond, but they will live if we do not. I am not living a lie. I am not marrying a man who does not worship the person that I am. You should not either."

There was a pause, and I adjusted the straps on the saddle, tightening them down around the horse so it wouldn't rub the animal. I attached the saddlebags she had leaned against a post and went to talk to the animals.

"He's a wily devil," the fiancée said to her. "He'll have your virtue, your soul, and leave you thinking it was your idea."

There was a lilt to her voice. "Or maybe it will be my idea. Maybe I'm tired of being tethered by things that mean nothing. Maybe I'll be the one to lead someone astray this time, Dom. I'm tired of this life. I do not live but simply exist. And it is exhausting."

He spit. "You will throw away your whole life for what?"

I could see them past the horses. I stroked their noses, letting them smell my breath and skin. Letting them know me. I had sugar cubes for them in my pockets, and they began to nuzzle it. I pulled one out for each and fed them.

"I'm not throwing away anything worth having. I'm not a broodmare or a shiny token to put on a shelf. I am a living, breathing woman. And I will have my adventures. It may not be with *that* coppery devil, but it will be. I will not go quietly into oblivion."

He grabbed her arm, and I was ready to intervene, but she snatched it away before hugging him tightly. She pulled away and gripped his head between her hands.

"I am only going to find his book. I will return, and we will find a way out of this. We both deserve to have our hearts full and happy. If I have to talk to the Ifrit, then so be it, but we will find a way out."

He hugged her to him. "Not that. We'll find another way. That damn Ifrit will have your soul quicker than that ginger demon."

I frowned at the horses. "I am not a demon or a devil. That's just mean-spirited and rude." I fed them another cube of sugar, and they nuzzled me happily. At least I'd made two friends.

Ekaterina strode up, vaulted onto her saddle, and turned the horse around. She tossed her dark braid over one shoulder and looked at me imperiously.

"Are you coming or not? We are wasting daylight."

I shook my head and pulled myself onto my own saddle. "After you, milady."

She rolled her eyes. "Cut the charm. I've had enough to last a lifetime."

"Your will be done."

WE RODE IN SILENCE for hours. I'd turned my ring back, so I wasn't hearing everything for miles. It could be very distracting. I hadn't learned much, except she felt trapped and sought a way out. I couldn't blame her for that. I felt bad for Dom, too. It couldn't be easy to be different, to love outside the bounds of what those you loved and respected did. He seemed like a good man and deserved to love who and how he wanted, just like Ekaterina had said.

I didn't think the book I was looking for would be of help. It was an ancient demonology text and would likely find more trouble than it would evade. But perhaps I could do something. Perhaps the Drake knew of something. I glanced at the afternoon sky to see a small dark dot in the distance. I knew it was him, could feel his presence in my mind. He was watching, my backup from a distance.

"What do you stare at so seriously?" she asked me from only a few feet away.

"Thinking, not staring."

"What troubles a man such as you?"

"Such as me? Again, with the scorn. What have I done to displease you so?"

She scowled darkly enough to scare away a demon, then smoothed her face. "Nothing. You have done nothing."

I patted the horse's neck and glanced away. "Then what? What has you in such a mood?"

"Nothing you can help me with."

"Why don't you try me? I've been known to help a damsel in distress on occasion."

She stared at me with huge blue eyes, and the air was too thin. I hadn't lied. I had a soft spot for damsels. I wasn't entirely sure she was a damsel, but she was definitely in distress. The odds were in her favor.

"And what will it cost me?"

"The words to tell me what is troubling you and perhaps a shared meal."

We were beside a creek, and she stopped the horse to jump down nimbly. I did the same, and we led the horses over to the water, tied their leads to a small tree, and allowed them to graze on the grass and drink their fill of water.

She pulled out bread and cheese, along with a few small tomatoes. When we'd fashioned sandwiches from the food, she began to talk. I listened quietly, allowing her to tell it all. When she was finally done and staring into the distance, I spoke.

"So, your families believe this prophecy means you two will join and change the world. But you do not believe this?"

She shook her head. "No. The prophecy states that a combination of the families will result in a world that is new. It doesn't say me. It doesn't say him. It could be my cousin, for all I know."

She has unbraided and rebraided her hair several times and was in the process of doing so again. I clucked my tongue at her and waved her over. She raised an ebony brow but came to sit in front of me.

I loosed her hair and combed through the wavy tresses with my fingers. "Tell me the exact wording of the prophecy if you can remember it."

"A combination, from the families Cooper and Vitoli two, will result in a world that is new," she spouted off with no delay.

I began to braid small sections of hair as we spoke, massaging her scalp as I went, speaking words of wisdom, hope, and clarity into the intricately knotted pieces as I did. She would require my help to release them.

"This prophecy, who made it?"

She leaned heavily against me for a moment, and I had a face full of her hair. She must use some sort of lavender soap for her hair because she smelled of lavender and sunshine. My heart sped up. *Slow down, idiot. We are not here to make conquests, nor does she wish to be conquered.*

"I don't know. It has been passed down for generations."

"Then why are they convinced it is to be you two? Couldn't it be the next generation?"

She glanced back at me over her shoulder, and it was all I could do not to lean in to taste her lips. But she hadn't given any indication she wanted that, or me. And what she'd said to the other one didn't really count. She'd been angry. She glanced at my mouth, and I had a brief instant of hope, but instead, she answered me.

"It could, but our parents have decided it is us. They feel the coming of the hundred-year comet on the eve of our shared birthdays is a sign. We are to be married on the day of our twenty-first year, under the hundred-year comet, on All Hallows Eve, with both families in attendance. Then have a three-day festival to celebrate of our joining and eventual world renewal."

I finished the final twisting braid and used her pin to hold it. She groaned as I rubbed her neck.

"That doesn't seem like much pressure on the two of you at all. So nice of your families to give you direction without making you feel like the fate of the world depended on you."

She laughed softly and reached up to touch her hair. "Oh my god. How many braids did you put in there?"

I stood up and dusted my pants off. "No idea. Enough. I wove wisdom, hope, and clarity into them. We'll figure something out," I said, reaching down to help her stand. "Let me think on it."

Her eyes met mine, and she looked very young without the hair. I took a step back from her and went to get the horses ready.

"How long do we have before sunset? I don't want to chance hurting the horses traveling after dark."

Her hand was on my shoulder, and I managed not to jump. "What's wrong? Something changed."

I shook my head and smiled at her. "Nothing wrong. Just thinking."

She frowned, and I knew she didn't believe me. *How do you tell an almost twenty-one-year-old that you are already two hundred and twenty-nine years old? If you can figure that out, tell me so I know as well.*

We rode on, and I let her dilemma roll around in my thoughts. What would make their families believe their prophecy was wrong or at least wasn't about them? They didn't want them to be miserable. They loved them. Was that not how families worked?

It had been so long since I'd had one it was hard to remember. I had the Drake and other friends, but my family was long gone. I'd been given a gift of longevity, but I was the only one with that gift in my family. It came with magic and joy but also with loss and responsibility. I'd missed laying my mother to rest, missed the birth of my nieces and nephews. So many lives had passed without knowing me or even about me.

My father cried when last I saw him; so happy was he to know I was alive. He'd died within hours of seeing me. I'd helped lay him to rest and left my homeland. I'd never see Ireland again without that sadness in my soul.

Ekaterina stopped us around the edge of a forest, with a stream on one side and a hill at our backs. She tied off the horses, fed them, and set up a fire before I even fully realized what was happening.

"My apologies. I am not normally so useless. I will try to find something to cook if you'd like."

She waved that idea off and motioned for me to sit. "I have beans and dried meat for soup. We can hunt for something tomorrow when the light is better. I started tea as well."

I pulled down my bed roll and pack before sitting down. The fire was warm and bright. The sky was full of stars, and the moon was only a sliver in the sky.

"What has you so pensive? Have you taken on my problems so fully you've lost yourself?"

My eyes lifted to her face, still young, but her eyes were full of something I couldn't describe. Like her ancestors were there just behind the blue depths, waiting for a time to speak.

"I feel old tonight."

She laughed. "You are young yet to feel old, sir. You can't be more than five and twenty."

"Alas, I am," I said, laying back to look at the stars. I noticed a shadow cross the sliver of the moon and land nearby. "And, alas, I must leave you to find a private spot."

She chuckled. "That creek water didn't sit well, I suppose. I'll listen for you; do not wander too far, or the forest folk might steal you away. They would love that ginger hair."

"Your will be done."

I heard her snort as I walked away into the woods.

"What is wrong?" I asked the Drake.

"Why must something be wrong? You have been gone for nigh on a fortnight, and you ask me what is wrong."

I sighed. "You have known where I was the entire time. Why have you chosen now to seek me out? Has something happened?"

"Who is your escort?" he asked, craning his neck as if he could see through the dense forest canopy.

"Are you simply curious? Is that why you risked being discovered?"

He swung his head around and glared at me with a huge red eye.

"You smell of lavender and Romani. Have you found another woman to entangle yourself with? Fyn, you are going to get us killed…"

"It's not like that," I told him as my face pulled into a scowl. "And what does a Romani smell like?"

He snorted hotly. "Like a lightning storm, magic, and temptation."

I glowered at him. "She's my guide to find the demonology book we need to end this infernal infestation. Do you remember that? The demon infestation?"

"I am not the one cavorting with females."

My vision went red, and I launched an ice-bolt at his stupid eye. He roared in response and snapped his massive jaws at me.

"You are an overgrown pair of boots! I am doing all the heavy work here. You fly around eating deer and cows while I have to do all the damned work."

"You!" he growled. "You think you are pulling the heavy load. I have lugged you around the world, and you aren't light. It's not like you have tried to make it easier. You gallivant and cavort and fornicate with every willing female, and then get me shot! And for what? You GAVE *away* the necklace."

"So we could get the book! We must get the book, or all this is for nothing!" I yelled with my arms thrown up.

I was pacing around and finally realized he wasn't talking anymore. I turned to find my new friend standing at the edge of the clearing we were in, staring with an open mouth. Her face was shocked. I glanced at Drake, and he looked contrite.

I sighed. "Ekaterina, this is Drake. Drake, Ekaterina," I said by way of introduction.

She snapped her mouth shut and strode over to me. She slapped me across the face with an open palm, and my mouth fell open. Drake laughed, but he stopped abruptly when she turned snapping eyes on him.

I was rubbing my cheek. "What was that for?"

"You have a dragon," she said, pointing to him.

"You struck me because I have a dragon? Madame, I do not understand."

Drake shook his head when I looked over at him. Neither of us understood what had just happened. His face looked as confused as I felt.

She fell to her knees in front of him and bowed her head. "Oh, great one, I have heard stories of you and yours. What do you require of me and mine?"

I lifted a brow and looked in askance at Drake. For his part, he remained confused and raised a shoulder in a shrug. He made a face and raised his forehands up in a gesture of confusion to match. She lowered her head to the ground in supplication.

I motioned for him to tell her to get up. He cocked his head to the side until I mumbled to tell her to get up.

"Rise, child. You need not prostrate yourself."

She sat back on her heels and looked at him in awe. I started to speak, and she glared at me hotly. I raised my hands and backed away. I gave Drake serious eye contact and nodded towards her. He smiled knowingly and nodded.

"We require your assistance, young one. But first, what stories have you heard of me?"

I shook my head and sat down on the ground in a huff. Stupid lizard. I listened somewhat patiently while she told him the first five stories. After the tenth, and one I was not even in, I practically levitated with impatience. He looked over and cleared his throat.

"Thank you for indulging me, little Katya. We require your assistance obtaining a book from the Stone Giants. I know Fyn has already spoken to you of it, but it would help us ever so much for you to help him locate it."

She beamed up at him and nodded. Her face was full of wonder and happiness. She turned to look at me, and that expression changed to anger. I scowled back at her.

"Thank you for your help, Drake. I think I can take it from here," I said without looking his way.

"You won't be coming with us?" she asked, crestfallen.

"Unfortunately, I will not be able to do so. That part of the mountain has proven too dense for me to navigate."

I thought she would cry; she was so sad. His own eyes became bleak, and I wanted to smack him. I thought about sending another ice bolt but didn't feel like having her look at me like I'd kicked a puppy, so I managed to stop myself.

"Drake, thank you again for a lovely evening and wonderful turn of events. You've been so helpful. Goodnight."

He snorted at me and bowed at the neck to Ekaterina before loping away to fly off. She watched him go, and I watched her face transform from wonder at him to fury at me.

"Why didn't you tell me you had a dragon?" she asked as she stalked up to me.

I watched her carefully. I didn't wish to be slapped again. When it didn't appear she would strike me further, I set off for our camp. She followed at a jog before catching me and stepping in front of me with an arm out.

I looked at her hand on my chest until she moved it. "I'll thank you to keep your hands to yourself, dear. I do not appreciate being struck, nor do I wish to repeat the performance. I will not put my hands on you, and I'd appreciate the same assurances from you."

I could have sworn I saw disappointment on her face but decided it was a trick of the light or her rapidly cycling moods. She was exhausting. It was why long-term relationships often failed, in my opinion. Emotions were just very tiring and burdensome. Have fun, move on. That was my motto, and it's worked up to now—with many happy encounters.

"You haven't answered me," she said when we reached the encampment.

"I didn't know that was a real question. Of course, I didn't tell you. I barely know you, and dragons aren't real."

Her face became mulish, and she pointed towards the sky, where he was flying back and forth in front of the sliver of a moon. Damned lizard.

"Mine own eyes have seen the truth. You cannot deny the majesty of the creature."

I snorted. "That is a walking, talking pair of boots. And a nice hat if I'm lucky."

Her face held outrage. "How dare you? He is beautiful and magical and wonderful."

I unfurled my bedroll and removed my boots and clothes to my undershirt and linen underpants. She sucked in a breath and turned away. Good. I took off the undershirt, too, and hung them all up on bushes to air out. I climbed in my bedroll and turned my backside to the fire to warm.

"He,"—I finally said— "is a giant pain in my ass. There is nothing majestic about a pain in your ass. I'm starting to wonder if you will be in that same category."

She sucked in a breath and managed to kick me in the head on her way by. I chuckled and snuggled down in my bedroll. She wouldn't be thinking any more whimsical thoughts about me now.

I glanced over my shoulder in time to see her slip into her own blankets. I laid my head down and, within seconds, was asleep.

My backside was cold and hadn't been a few seconds ago. The fire must have gone out. I cracked open my eyes to see the fire steaming. That's not right. I opened them wide to see my travel companion with an empty bucket and a malicious smile on her face.

"Why did you put out the fire?"

"You slept through breakfast, and it's time to go. I didn't think you'd want to leave a fire going once we left."

"I would have been fine to wait until the sun fully lit the sky, love. There is not enough light to keep the horses from breaking a leg."

She allowed her lip to slide out and rubbed at her eyes as if to rub away tears. What a little brat. How had I ever thought she was beautiful or nice. "Don't call me love."

"Have you decided then you do not require my assistance with your problem?"

Her nostrils flared, and she sat back on the ground. Clearly, she'd forgotten about that. She sighed heavily and rubbed at her face in earnest.

"You really are an infuriating man."

"Sadly, you are not the first to tell me so. Not even the second. I take that for a no. You do still want my help?"

She nodded. "Yes. I still need your help."

"Marvelous. You will have to turn around while I get out of this roll. I am not dressed for inspection."

She turned around but grumbled. "I've seen men before."

"You were the one turning away last night. That means you must also turn away this morning."

"So you say. What have you thought of to help me?"

"You may turn around," I told her as I moved to put my bedroll to rights. "I must admit it is a conundrum for me."

She was putting her things to rights, as well, and listening. I started putting things on the horse.

"We have a few options. We can make your families believe you are completely incompatible," she started to speak, and I held up a finger to halt her. "We could convince them the prophecy is about some other poor saps. You could simply refuse. Or, and this is my personal favorite, you could convince them the prophecy doesn't mean what they think it means."

She stood beside her horse, staring at me. I didn't feel the look on her face properly projected the feelings of awe and gratitude my ideas should have engendered. When she laughed, I shrugged and swung onto the back of my horse.

"Let's go, Precious," I told him and patted his neck.

"Why are you calling that horse precious?"

I looked back at her with a smile in my eyes. "Mostly because it is his name."

She snorted. "His name is horse; we do not name the work animals. It seems to confuse them."

I laughed, and she bristled. "That's because he already has a name, and if you call him by another, he thinks you speak to another," I told her and paused. "You know, there are a few more options. We could fake your death."

"Why do you think his name is Precious? Fake my death, how?"

Precious snorted softly but continued to plod on. "He told me his name was Precious," I told her. "It wouldn't be that hard. I could say you fell into a ravine, or wolves tore you apart, or you drowned."

"Been planning this, have you?" she asked with a look of mild shock.

"No, love, those are off the top of my head," I told her, laughing softly. "It will have to be something with no body left. Otherwise, they will expect me to produce one. I'll not be killing another to get you out of a marriage when you can simply say no."

"Two things, Mr. Farrel. First, I cannot simply say no. They will never allow that; I have no choice. Second, the horse told you, his name? You're saying he can talk?"

I smiled over at her and watched her irritation turn to confusion. I had that kind of smile. My winsome face and sunny smile had gotten me out of many a sticky situation. They had, however, gotten me into more than they'd gotten me out of. But that was a tale for another day.

"Did you hear him talking? 'Course not," I said, and her confusion began to abate until I finished. "I can hear him in my mind. She won't tell me her name; says you don't like me, and if you don't trust me, she won't either."

She looked down at her horse and back up to me, trying to decide how much to believe. She met my eyes, and I saw the moment she decided to ignore it. I nodded.

"And, love, you always have a choice. They may not be good choices, but they are choices nonetheless. You could always run away."

"I have nothing," she said, looking off into the distance. The profile of her features in the rising morning sun was beautiful, something you would want to stare at in a museum. She caught me staring and glowered, ruining the effect. "Don't call me love."

We rode silently for hours, and I watched the idea of leaving take root in her head. It was the only option I felt would work, aside from faking her death, but I'd known she wouldn't take that option. Though running was something I hadn't expected her to agree to either. She didn't seem much like a runner.

When we reached our destination, her shoulders were stiff, her jaw rigid, and her resolve set. She waved up towards a misty clearing.

"The brothers."

I nodded to her. She took Precious's reins from my hands and waved me onward. I began to stride forward but turned to look back at her.

"I'll wait here."

I nodded once in acknowledgment and went on. Once I made it to the mist, I offered a prayer of blessing and asked permission to enter the sacred place. A small opening appeared, and I stepped through to have it close behind me. The pillars stood sound and strong. I went to the widest of them and knelt before it.

I engaged my rings of clarity, wisdom, and luck before reciting my incantation for discovery. Then repeated my incantation twice more, and with a final whispered, so I have said, so mote it be. A soft glow began inside the pillar.

I edged around until I could tell which crevice it emanated from and took a deep breath. I wasn't keen on snakes, but as cold as it was, there shouldn't be any, right? I reached into the opening, barely large enough for my hand, and felt around while I prayed nothing bit me.

I finally felt something and grasped it. But there were two things tucked into the space. I pulled out the first, a slim tome that was not the demon text I required and in a language I would need to study further to understand. The second wouldn't come out. I had to work very hard, and my knuckles were scraped to pieces when I had it out. I was careful not to allow my blood to touch the text. It was my demonology book, and the last thing I needed was to accidentally summon something or have a conduit into my soul from something within.

I asked the sacred place for permission to take the books, and the mist opened for me again. I smiled and tucked the demonology tome into the pocket of my pants. The other text wouldn't fit with it, so I held it in my hands. I strode up to Ekaterina and the horses with a broad grin.

The look on her face was at odds with my feelings of success.

"You got it?" she asked, eyes only for the book in my hands.

I nodded and waved the book in my hands at her before answering. "Yes. Just where it was supposed to be."

"Good," she said just before I felt a white-hot pain in the back of my head.

"You seemed sincere, but I need this more than you," she said as she took the book out of my hands. "They will never allow me to leave."

The last thing I heard before oblivion took me was her apology—followed by cool lips pressed against my forehead and then softly against my own mouth.

"I am sorry. Perhaps we will meet again, you coppery devil."

Devil, Demon, Guardian

Fynbar & Ekaterina

I rode like the devil was after me. And truth be told, I was worried he might be. Fynbar Farrel was going to be furious when he awoke. I'd stolen his book, the horse, and his belongings. I'd left him the clothes on his back and the amulet he'd paid me with. I'd felt guilty enough taking the book and his packs, but I didn't know what was in them, and he might have something there to track me.

He used magic, had a dragon, and had a face that haunted my dreams. The horse we'd rented to him was being stubborn. If Fynbar was to be believed, the horse's name was Precious, and he was bucking and trying desperately to get free. When we were halfway back home, I finally let him go. If the damn thing wanted to kill his fool self, there was nothing I could do. I couldn't keep fighting him.

I glanced back at the horse, and he whinnied at us. My own horse nickered back but continued on without slowing. I patted her neck and wondered if Fyn really could hear her. She was a strong horse, but I'd have to slow down soon. She wasn't meant for speed but distance and hard work.

When we'd left both the man and the horse far behind, I stopped at a small stream to let her drink and graze. I threw a blanket over her and sat down to look at the book I'd taken. The cover was so old, the words on the outside were worn away.

I took a deep breath and opened the cover.

My heart sank to my toes, tears stung my eyes, and I thought my chest would collapse inward. I flipped to another page and then another and another. It didn't matter. They were all blank.

Fat tears dripped off the tip of my nose, and then it began to rain. I'd always had an affinity for the weather; it often affected my moods, and sometimes, though I never told anyone, I thought my moods might affect it. Today was such a day. There'd been not a cloud in the sky before now.

I closed the book hurriedly and pushed it down into my pack. Although, with nothing but blank pages, why I bothered was beyond me. I sat in the rain, staring at nothing until it was too dark to go on. The horse came over to nudge me, and I pulled out a ration of grain for her to eat.

I was too despondent to eat, so I found a canopy of trees out of the rain and leaned back to rest my burning eyes. I hadn't slept well. Dreams of fiery kisses and hot grey eyes had made me toss and turn. I'd been so mad I'd almost thrown the icy water on the devil this morning, only barely managing to restrain myself. It might have been worth it to see him scantily clad, wet, and mad. Would have served him right. I sighed inwardly. And yet, I am the one who offered betrayal.

I closed my eyes against the feelings of regret and loss. He would not have helped me. They were surely empty words meant to placate an unhappy woman. *Absolutely. Surely? Mayhap.*

It matters not, Ekaterina. As he said, you always have a choice. And you made your choice.

I let sleep pull me under and fell into dreams of the copper demon, startling grey eyes, and muscular arms.

The soft nibbling at my ear was nice until I smelled the breath attached to it. And then there was the long tongue in my ear that seemed to lick my brain.

"Once more," I heard Drake's impatient voice. "Once more, Precious. He isn't moving yet. Are you certain he is alive?" There was a silence and then the tongue was moving back toward my brain. "Oh, don't get fussy. I'm simply worried about the idiot," he huffed.

I brushed the horse's mouth from my ear and sat up. "I'm alive," I said and grabbed my head. "Although this aching head makes me wish for death. What did that shrew hit me with?"

Precious nudged a branch to me, and Drake boomed out a laugh. "I told you one of them was going to kill you. You would do well to listen to me more often."

I scowled up at my dragon familiar, who was flapping his enormous wings to remain above the trees but within distance of shouting down at me.

"Is there a clearing we can go to so I can stop wiping dirt out of my eyes? My head hurts abysmally, and you're creating an environment of discord."

He rolled his large red eyes and swung his dark head to the right. "Yes, lord cranky pants. Just down the mountain and to the west."

I scowled again and, when it hurt even more, smoothed my face. When I moved to get up, the amulet I'd paid Ekaterina with fell to the ground. I picked it up and tucked it into my pants pocket along with the demonology book. They fit snugly, and I buckled the pocket back closed. The other book was missing.

I sighed but managed to get myself into the saddle to let Precious take us to Drake. He was pacing around the large clearing with a lake in the center of it. It was similar to the one we'd hidden in after stealing the damn necklace not long ago.

"What did you do to that lovely creature to make her brain you?" he demanded.

I slid down from Precious and let him wander the clearing. He went to the water and drank his fill before grazing on the sweet grass surrounding the pond. He was content.

"Me? I did nothing. I guess the book's draw was too much," I told him.

"Why? It will do nothing for her. Unless"—he asked suspiciously—"is she fighting demons?"

I snorted. "No, and she isn't marrying one either."

At his look of confusion, I filled him in on her problems and her interest in the book, which I'd learned from the overheard conversation.

"And why did she believe your book would help her? Didn't you tell her it was a demonology volume?"

"Why would I tell her that? She was clearly untrustworthy!" I told him, throwing my arms up. "Look what she did when she didn't know."

He chuckled. "She's a bit of a spitfire, eh."

I snarled. "A hellion, more like. She hit me! On the head! With a limb!"

"Probably the only way she could get you to shut up."

I shook my fist at him. "Well, she got the wrong book," I said, pulling out the demonology text.

He swung his large red eyes around to stare at me. "What wrong book? There was more than one?"

I grinned up at him triumphantly. "Yes. And she took the other one."

"Does that one have the answers we need?"

"I haven't looked at it yet," I told him, sitting down with the book. I opened the pages and frowned. "The pages are blank."

He made a huffing noise, the horse chuffed, and I flipped the book over to look at the back. There was nothing different there. I closed my eyes and said a silent prayer to Apollo for guidance and help. A word popped into my head. I said it while moving my hand over the book, and the cover transformed. I opened the book to find the pages full of ancient Latin text.

How fortunate I was knowledgeable of Latin. I read through the text and sighed forlornly. I would have to retrieve the other book before I could put down the demon rebellion in the Americas.

"What say you, young'un? Are we ready?" Drake asked.

I sighed again. "No. I'll need the other one. I'll have to get it back from the hellion. Can you see if you can find her? I'll start riding towards their settlement. Hopefully, we'll catch her before she gets back."

"Surely you don't need..."

I gave him hard eyes, and he pulled back abruptly. "This one is written in code," I told him, holding the volume up. "And the other is the codex. So, yes, I must have it."

"Why did you dally with the girl?" he whined.

I gaped at him. "I did no such thing. That little thief let me get the books, waited for me to return, hit me over the head, and stole what she thought I'd found."

I mounted Precious and swung him around. He tossed his head and pranced like a prize stallion. I patted his neck appreciatively. Drake pumped his wings and began to rise.

"I should wallop her when I find her. If she were a man, I most assuredly would."

He made a humming sound. It was meant to be low and unobtrusive but was instead a great thrumming sound that reverberated through me.

"Stop it, you overgrown gecko, before you cause a landslide or an earthquake."

He glanced back apologetically and then scowled darkly. "T'would serve you right for even thinking of beating that sweet girl."

I snorted. "Nothing sweet about her. She's a deceitful little wretch, and when I find her, I will throttle her."

"I'll bet you our next treasure you do not," he laughed mockingly. "In fact, I'll bet you this one and the next that you don't even yell at her."

I chuckled. "Easiest treasure I'll ever take from another."

His booming laugh echoed around me as he flew away. "So, it will be."

I scowled after him and urged Precious into a run. It wouldn't be too hard to catch up. If nothing else, Drake could detain her until I arrived.

I repeated an incantation I'd learned only this season from a beautifully wicked Witch in Bogota to infuse Precious with vigor and stamina. It pulled from the Chaos of the forest and allowed the debt to be paid by myself instead of the innocent horse. This was my first use of the spell; it would remain to be seen how it affected me.

The other thing I did was seek out the magic I infused the braids I put in her hair with. It was my Chaos and thus called to me. I'd never have found it if it had been more than a few days old, but the magic was still very strong. I located the thread, and we raced toward the tingling warmth of familiar Chaos magic.

We rode hard for an hour before I noticed Drake circling an area not far away. The sky opened up at that moment, crying tears of pity and sorrow down upon us. I could not have told you why I felt the sky's sorrow, but it was a palpable thing weighing me down.

Drake circled one last time before flying off to his hiding place. Or maybe to find a nice cow for dinner; hard to tell with him. I rode up to a small creek, a grazing horse, and a sleeping woman. I let Precious stop, and he whinnied to the mare. She tossed her head, and I let him prance over to her. *Hmmm.*

I slipped from the saddle, and still Ekaterina did not wake. I walked over to her after telling Precious they must stay close. He ignored me in favor of the mare nickering at him. I rolled my eyes.

I pulled her pack over to me, going through it to find my book inside. The pages bloomed with words when I flipped them open, saying the same spellword. I glanced through it enough to see the book was more than just a codex, although it was definitely that, too.

I tucked the small book into my back pocket, what I should have done before, and stood undecided about what to do next. She was still asleep. She looked like a drowned cat. I sighed; it made my heart a little warmer. Little hellion deserved a bit of bad luck.

I bent over to shake her awake, but she only groaned her brow furrowing. Was something wrong with the little wretch? I nudged her with my foot, and she tipped over, arms flopping down.

Oh gods, is she dead?

I knelt down to touch her cautiously. Her skin was cold and very pale. I touched her neck to feel her pulse. It was a frantic, fluttering thing under my fingers. I pulled up my second sight to see some dark essence coming from the book and feeding off her aura. I rolled my eyes and looked up at the heavens. *Not that kind of bad luck!*

I felt Apollo roll his own metaphysical eyes, and the word to close the connection between her and the book floated in front of my eyes. It was nice to have a direct link to the god of knowledge, as long as he wasn't on a bender.

The connection cut, she breathed more easily, and her color returned to something resembling normal. The rain slowed and finally eased to a fine mist. I pulled out my tent, set it up, managed to get her inside on the bedroll, and covered with blankets.

She shivered uncontrollably, and I piled the rest on top of her. I felt sleep pulling me under, too, and I lay back to rest my eyes. Suddenly, I was dizzy with exhaustion. The world spun uncontrollably, and darkness descended.

I woke snuggled under blankets in a tent and had no idea how I had gotten there. There was a warm fire crackling outside the open tent flap. My bag was gone. *Damnit.* I had a feeling I knew who the tent belonged to.

The rain had stopped. And when I crawled out of the tent, I was face to face with Fynbar Farrel's handsome, scowling face. My pack sat beside him on the ground and my horse nuzzled his neck like a traitor. He reached up to absently stroke her nose but glared at me.

"Welcome to the world of the living, Ms. Cooper. I am ecstatic you could join me."

I finished crawling out of the tent to look at the star-filled sky. The moon was a small sliver of silver shining in the sky. A wolf howled in the distance and a shiver ran down my spine as I looked up into hard grey eyes.

"Mr. Farrel," I said hesitantly as I sat down in front of the fire opposite him.

He lifted a coppery brow, devastating my concentration and resolve as the firelight flickered over his stubbled face. It simply wasn't fair for a man to be so fair.

"Is that all you have to say for yourself? Mr. Farrel," he mimicked. "As if you did not just brain me, leave me for dead, and STEAL my book!"

I bit my lip and lowered my eyes in a show of regret.

"You are not sorry in the least. You can stop pretending. And what did it get you?"

My eyes lifted to his, and I didn't bother trying to look regretful or repentant. I did, in fact, attempt to put a bit of impudence in them. His own reflected back the firelight, making them look like there were flames in his eyes. It was disconcerting.

"I got nothing!" I spat at him. "The pages were blank. You also got nothing. I hope the fate of the world wasn't hanging on those pages."

He laughed sardonically and looked skyward. "You've no idea, little hellion. None. And now you've slowed me even more. I can only hope things have not degenerated more since I've been gone."

I snorted, and his eyes snapped back to mine. The flames dancing there returned and were even more disconcerting. How was he doing that? I moved, his eyes followed me, and the flames remained.

"Are you damned, then?"

The eyebrow lifted again. "Suppose that would depend on who you ask. I told you I would help you. Why did you steal from me?"

At last, I felt genuine regret, which angered me and put more irascibility in my eyes. How dare he make me feel bad for taking care of myself?

"As if you would have helped me. What would you require as payment? I have nothing to give except myself, which just takes me from one unwanted man's bed into another's. I'm already selling the right to look at my body. I won't sell the right to touch it too."

He drew back from me as if I'd slapped him. He shook his head slowly. "I asked for nothing. I required nothing. I was simply willing to help ya. I feel sorry for ya, A mhurinin. If you've ne'er had another simply befriend ya."

My brows drew down, and I felt a stinging in my eyes and nose. *Damn him!* "How was I to know?"

"Use your insight, girl. Can ya not tell when another is dishonest? Open your shields and look at their aura."

I frowned. "I...I don't know. I've never done that before. I...can usually tell when people mean to hurt me, but not always."

He sighed and stood up to pace. "You've ne'er been taught to use your magic then?"

I shook my head, confused. "I read my cards, palms, futures, tea leaves, but that isn't magic."

He stopped pacing to stare at me. "Are you daft? Of course, it's magic. Who taught you that? What else can you do?"

I sat back, my neck craning to keep him in sight. "Sit down, please. I. I'm sorry I took your book. I can see you didn't mean me harm. I don't know what else. I didn't realize that was really magic."

He sat down across from me and narrowed his eyes. "How did you not?"

I shrugged. "I've always been able to do it. I know the others do something similar..."

He was shaking his head. "No. They do not. You have the gift. They are reading the room. Doing something quite different. I imagine you see images of the things you say in your mind," he said, and I nodded. It was true.

"I thought as much. The others read the body language of their customer. Maybe not your sister. I couldn't tell. She has gifts but perhaps not the same as you. The babe as well."

My mouth fell open, and I stared at him. "Bohdan? How do you know?"

He smirked at me. "It matters not. I know. He will be highly intuitive, persuasive, and charismatic. He will draw others to him, and he will lead."

I smiled for the first time. It was a good thought, a comforting thought. "Will you still help me?"

He scowled darkly, and the night seemed darker, more ominous. "I'm not sure I should. You've not proven worthy."

I was chagrined by his words and my deeds. "I've apologized. What else..."

He cut me off with a harsh motion. "I told you it was not like that. I meant that. I simply must take care of my business first. Can you hold on a bit longer?"

My brow furrowed in thought. "The wedding isn't for two moons yet. Dom is in no hurry, and we cannot marry sooner, so I think we can safely say I can wait that long."

He nodded once, and his hot eyes fell on my face, making my breath catch, my chest tighten, and my skin flush. I leaned forward and couldn't think of anything but what his lips on my skin would feel like. *What the hell? My life is in chaos, and I've lost my mind over a copper-haired devil.* I shook my head at myself in disgust.

He leaned back slightly and crossed his arms over his broad chest. "Then I will take care of my business with haste and return to take care of yours. But for tonight, we must get a bit of rest."

I looked behind me at the tent and then back to him with lifted brows. "It's not a very large tent, sir."

He shook his head. I'll sleep out here. You take the tent."

I frowned, looking at his wan face. His freckles were standing out starkly against his pale face. He didn't look well.

"What is wrong with you? Are you sick?"

He shook his head with a sigh. "No, love, I've just overtaxed myself. Nothing a bit of rest won't remedy."

His eyes were dull, creases present around them, and he grew more haggard as I watched. I was suddenly apprehensive.

"I think we can safely share the tent. Come on. I'll split the blankets with you."

His eyes drooped as he shook his head. "No. I'll not..."

"Stop arguing, or I'll just drag you in after you fall asleep. I do not think it would be a pleasant trip."

He struggled into a standing position, staggered, and stumbled into the tent. He fell down and didn't move again. It did not appear there would be a problem with us sharing the space. I checked to be sure he was alive and covered him with one of the blankets. His skin was cold, so I gave him another and snuggled up close to him. The temperature had dropped after the rain. It was rather cold out, and his clothes were damp.

I clucked my tongue but simply covered us with the blankets and pressed my warmth to him. He was firm and unmoving. His large body was heavy, dead weight. I wrapped myself around him and fell asleep with his chest as a pillow. It was a singularly satisfying experience.

When I awoke hours later, he was gone. The necklace was around my neck, and a note was atop my pack. I felt a sense of loss as I packed up the camp and set off for home. The ruby necklace glinted and sparkled in the sunlight as I rode toward home to await the ginger demon's return. To save my life. To change my fate. Perhaps he was to be a ginger guardian.

Endings, Beginnings, Forever

Fynbar & Ekaterina

"You are sure you must go back for the girl?" Drake asked forlornly. "Could we not just allow fate to remain as it may?"

"You met her, you overgrown handbag. You would leave her to marry a man she does not love. A man who does not equal her? A man who would not appreciate her splendid...ah...self?"

Who knew dragons could raise supercilious brows? "You are a fool."

I was seated on his back, nestled between his great, scaled, feathered wings. He looked back at me, his long neck high above me, his head turned. I grinned up at him and kicked my heels back into his body. "Giddup."

He snorted out a hot breath, ruffled himself, and made me grip him tightly with my knees. There was no holding on. He tossed his head and ran to take off.

We'd finished our business in the Americas. The demon uprise had been all but quashed. It would take us almost two days to return to her mountain home, but I had promised and would not break that promise. As it was, we were going to be cutting things very close. It was three days from All Hollow's Eve, and we were halfway across the world. Lucky for me, Drake was a tireless devil.

I buckled myself into the straps I'd put on him. They kept me from falling off if I fell asleep. They were attached to him and held my legs in place. I'd safely slept atop his back many times with this contraption.

"How is our friend?" he asked, his head swiveled around to look back at me again.

I pulled the warm fleece of my jacket back to stare down. A pair of small eyes stared back at me from underneath a top hat. A minuscule pair of goggles, an orange cockatiel feather, and tiny playing cards rode the brim of the purple felt hat. The hat sat atop the head of a lightning bug familiar of the Witch I'd just helped in America.

"How are you, Thibideaux?" I asked.

"Jus' fine, mon amie. How much longer we gon' be traveling? You know I leave at midnight."

I looked up at the sky and grinned. "It will take us two days travel time to get to her. Unless you know another way?"

He sucked his teeth and then blew out a breath.

"Well now, boy, I might just know a way. You got any of your lady loves things?"

I scowled down at him as Drake jiggled us around, laughing, I suspected. "She is not my lady love."

"Then why you need ole Thibideaux? You either gon' get there or not. If she ain't the one, then why you care so much?"

I opened and closed my mouth. Thought about her married to some man who would love her but not be in love with her, living a life of servitude to her family, and changing the world without me. Then I rolled my eyes at my own thoughts.

Thibideaux chuckled. "What ya got dat belong to her?"

"I don't really have anything that belongs to her. However," I said, pulling out a tarot card she'd given me, "I have this card she gave me."

"If it reminds you of her enough, it will be fine. We can use it to pull us after we go through the door."

I frowned at the little lightning bug. "What door? I know of no door. How?"

"You Witches always thinkin' you know so much. There's a door through the InBetween. As long as you have something to connect to."

I held up the card, thinking of Ekaterina in her dance costume, and flushed with heated recollection. I cleared my throat and fidgeted.

"I think this will work."

Thibideaux laughed. "Seems like she made quite the impression. You need to head to the bayou." I hooked a thumb in the opposite direction we were going. "Back dat' a way."

Drake was already turning back. We weren't far from the bayou as we'd just flown over the area. Thibideaux was chuckling softly at the rapid beating of my heart.

"You nervous, boy?"

I shrugged my shoulders slightly. "I hope not to be too late. And I am tired after my part of the battle. There was much Chaos being thrown around."

Drake bobbed his head. "Yes, but I did most of the heavy lifting this time, lazy Witch."

I scowled. "You may have blown things up with your fireballs, you overgrown salamander, but I did just as much work. You think those demons stood in groups for fun? Mind magic is even harder on those slimy brains," I said tiredly. "How long before we get there?"

Drake looked back at me worriedly, and I made a face. "Don't look at me like that, lizard boy. I am simply tired."

His expression did not change. "You have at least an hour. Unless you are not required to be awake when we pass through."

Thibideaux shook his little head. "Sorry, mon amie, you must needs be awake for the portal to function."

I nodded and leaned back against the supplies stacked behind me. "An hour it is, then."

They managed to find an open area to land Drake's substantial frame. They also waited until they located the doorway to wake me. It was a two-hour nap, and I felt only marginally better. When I'd said the mind magic was draining, that was only scratching the surface. Mind magic was physically, mentally, and emotionally draining.

Performing mind magic on demons was so very much worse. Their brains were full of oily thoughts, nefarious plans, and gruesome torture scenes. It was difficult to guard against invasion while constantly pushing to invade. It was exhausting, draining, and depleting.

I yawned so wide it made my jaw hurt. "Ouch," I said, rubbing my face. "What's next?"

Thibideaux was floating around in front of an opening. Not exactly a door, but moss hanging between colossal trees shaped like a massive entryway. No matter where you were from, it looked like a doorway, and according to Thibideaux, it was.

I rubbed at my gritty eyes and scrubbed my hands over my face in an attempt to wake up. It was twilight within the canopy of the trees, but it couldn't be more than noon.

"What must I do, little friend?"

"As you walk through the doorway, you gon' think about your sweetheart while holding that card. Don't let the thoughts of her lessen. You must focus on her to go to her. Otherwise, mon amie, you might end up anywhere or anytime."

"Are you not coming with us?"

He shook his head. "No, this is what I was meant to do. You will be there in time to help her decide, and I will go find another to help. You have your own familiar at work."

Drake rolled his eyes. "He is more familiar than I if one must be categorized as such."

Thibideaux cackled, and I snorted. "Do you know what would be helpful, you oversized, mouthy pair of boots? If you could make yourself smaller."

He snorted out a puff of hot smoke and swung his tail toward my head. I managed to duck in time to miss it. Thibideaux laughed so hard he dropped in the air, and I barely managed to catch him before he hit the boggy ground.

"I must bid you au revoir, mon amies. Be kind to one another," he said, drifting away.

I watched him go sadly. He'd been a massive help during the fights and had just given me a way to bypass days of travel. I looked over at Drake, who was watching me cautiously.

"What?"

He shook his large head, eyes heavy-lidded and concerned. "You are still exhausted."

I shrugged off his concern. "No more than you, I'd wager. You worked harder than I, after all."

He chuckled and followed me toward the portal. "So, I did. What shall we do if I do not make it through your portal?"

I jerked my head around. "What do you mean?"

"I am unsure I will fit in your doorway. In fact, I am positive I will not. Shall I meet you there?"

I looked at the door and back at him. As large as it was, it was still too small for my very large friend. Why had I not seen this before? Why had we never tried to find a way to make his bulk smaller?

"You are tired and only a mortal," he responded to my look.

At my opened mouth, he chuckled.

"Yes, only human, after all. Despite your years of living, you are still mortal and subject to the laws of nature, science, and even divinity."

I harrumphed, and he laughed harder. I'd never been one to let laws or humanity stop me from accomplishing what needed to be done. I often flouted those very things, inserting my own logic and beliefs in their place.

"I suppose meeting us there is the best I can hope for if you cannot come with me. It has been long since we were parted in this way. Can you not simply come to me when I arrive?"

He snorted, a tendril of smoke flowing along with the sound. "No. You know I am still bound by the mortal realm as I have never died. I am not able to…"

I held up my hand, nodding. "Yes, yes. I just thought perhaps you had learned something new since the last time. What with meeting new realm traveling familiars and whatnot."

He growled, and the leaves trembled over my head. I simply stared at him. His antics had never brought fear to my heart, one of the many reasons we worked together.

"Master Thibideaux has died, dies every day. He is afforded more leeway than I. My apologies if a fire-breathing, flying, magic-resistant familiar is not enough for one such as the great Fynbar Farrel. I will try to grow to match your humble renown."

"You don't have to become cross. I was simply asking. I meant no disrespect."

It was his turn to harrumph. He nudged me when I walked by him, so I stumbled. I turned to glare at him with upraised arms.

"Get your bag. At least the purse."

I scowled. "It's not a purse. It is a satchel for carrying the things I require."

"Also known as a purse," he stated flatly.

"Fine. Whatever. You are a giant lobcock, sir dragon, and I am done with you."

He blustered. "I will show you my…"

"No!" I cut him off with a raised hand while I walked the few steps toward the portal. "It is not literal, you great bag of air. If I do nothing else, I will teach you to understand insults and sarcasm."

"Bag," he told me, tossing it into the back of me. I stumbled again, almost falling into the doorway before I righted myself.

"You are determined to rid yourself of me, are you?" I asked while I pulled the satchel over my head.

"No. I simply didn't want to hear your caterwauling if you forgot it. You whine endlessly when things do not go as you plan. You have your ladyloves' card?"

"She is not my ladylove," I ground out, holding up the card.

"Ah, mayhap not, but you wish she was. You jackanapes."

I raised a brow as I settled the bag and my clothes around me. He was catching on, after all. I nodded in acknowledgment, and he smiled, pleased with himself.

I fixed Ekaterina's lovely features in my mind, held the card she'd given me, and took a deep breath before stepping through the doorway. I heard Drake's voice just before my body was enveloped in warmth.

"Godspeed, my friend."

The tingling warmth spread to envelop me fully. My nerves were alight with excitement and enervation. *It felt like being surprised, made ready to fight, and then finding out it was a mistake. That alive feeling just before, when every fiber of who you are is ready and moving towards the goal of keeping you alive. There are other times when this feeling is alive in you, but those are for less delicate ears.*

My blood was thrumming, my nerve endings alive, my breathing ragged, and my thoughts tried to float away. I dragged them back to Ekaterina, and the feelings became more pronounced. I'd not thought that possible, but it felt as if I would slip my skin and be nothing but soul and emotions. I managed to take two steps and stumbled into her family's club.

I was on fire, and the object of my heart was on the stage. She was dressed in scarves, each tied in such a way to hide what my eyes craved, what all our eyes evidently craved by the shouts from the audience. She would pull one from herself and twirl it with the music every few seconds, and I both worried and hoped she would soon run out of scarves to pull.

The patrons were cheering with each and tucked coins and gems into her remaining scarves and into the small collection hat on the edge of the stage. She nodded to me and continued to dance.

I bought a drink; this might be the longest song I'd ever heard in my life. I downed the dark liquor, and my blood continued to boil. My hands itched to touch her skin; my thoughts would not be swayed from her. I noticed the glint of the ruby necklace nestled between her breasts and heard the siren song.

I began to walk forward, hearing the haunting melody, feeling the unmistakable draw, unable to stop myself. I tossed four men and one woman out of the way and ended up before her. She stared down at me with huge, liquid eyes of deepest blue. One corner of her lips raised in a smile just before a chair came crashing down on my back. I held up a finger and turned to address the room. There was a circle around me, three with blades and one with a gun. I zeroed in on the firearm and went to dispatch the competition.

I waded through the room like liquid silver, drawing heavily on the lust-perfumed Chaos filling the room. I snatched the gun from the surprised man's hands and swung my elbow toward the side of his head. He went down with a thud. The weapon wasn't even loaded. I tucked it in the back of my trousers and turned to find the two gentlemen and one gentlewoman with knives surrounding me. They had no intention of doing this fairly. *Fine, neither did I.*

I used the mind magic I'd been throwing around so cautiously with the demons at the three, turning their rage and anger into something less destructive. They fell on each other with impassioned embraces. It would wear off before they could do anything they might regret, but it only enhanced what was already there, so maybe they wouldn't regret anything.

The woman became more enraged and approached me with a wicked two-foot blade, one smooth edge and one jagged. It was a knife for killing, plain and simple, and she was very skilled with it.

I managed to dodge the first two attacks, but in the third, she buried the blade in my arm, deep enough to stick in the bone. It is likely what saved my life, as she was unable to get it back out without sawing and working the blade. I managed to get behind her and put an arm around her throat while she continued working the blade. Eventually, she lost consciousness and fell to the floor. I fought the others in a frenzy.

I honestly don't remember the end of the fights, only standing in front of Ekaterina, chest heaving, on my knees, and imploring her with my eyes to have me. She bent over, still covered completely, and laid her hands on my cheeks. Her lips didn't move, but her eyes were full of sparkling joy.

I followed her into her tent and stared at her beautiful face while she called me six different kinds of fool and sewed up my arm. I wasn't sure when the knife had finally been removed, but the resulting wound was deep and spanned the length of my bicep. That arm would likely be useless for a while.

She hummed as she worked, and I felt a cold, stinging sensation with each stitch. I also felt the wound healing as she alternated between humming and scolding me. My eyes never left her face, and I couldn't begin to tell you what was happening around us.

"What have you decided?" I asked when she was halfway done.

"You are an idiot," she replied without missing a beat.

I frowned, raising my other hand with its bruised and scraped knuckles to her face. She glanced up at me but left my hand in place. I ran my thumb across her soft cheek and felt the world tilt.

"I feel as if that is not a new conclusion for you. What have you decided about your future?"

She bit her lip, and her face became troubled, uncertain. "What would you have me do? I am bound to these people. I have responsibilities you cannot possibly know."

I swallowed thickly. My heart beat erratically in my chest, and pain blossomed there to streak outward, ending in my belly. I suffered a distinct and complete feeling of loss so sudden my breath was gone and my thoughts scattered.

Her eyes held mine, and I slowly moved closer to her face, to her lips. "One kiss. And if you do not wish to be with me, I will leave you to your family and your responsibilities. I will darken your door no more."

She lifted a finger, pressing it to my mouth, stopping my movement forward. I felt heartbroken and began to move away from her. She dropped the needle and gripped my hair tightly in her fisted hand.

"I said nothing, you ginger demon. Do not give in so easily. I have a distinct desire to taste your mouth, to feel your lips on mine, to press my aching body to your own. But I have a question."

My breath shuddered to a halt, and my thoughts were once again strewn about like leaves in the fall winds. I could think of nothing but her words and the images those words inspired. I could do naught but nod slightly as she still had a ferocious grip on my hair.

"Will you leave me stranded here after having my body? Will you desert me to my fates? Will you use me and escape on the back of your dragon?"

I smiled against her finger and pressed a kiss to the interfering appendage.

"I would sooner leave this earth than you behind. I could no sooner leave you again than I could my own soul. We are connected, you and I. We are..."

She pressed her finger more firmly to my lips, effectively hushing me.

"We barely know one another. You cannot seriously be professing love to me."

I allowed my desire for her to fill my eyes. She drew in a breath of surprise and ran her finger over my mouth. I raised a brow.

"How long is an appropriate amount of time to know you are in love with someone? A week, a month, a year...an hour?"

"I barely know you," she said instead of answering.

"What is it you would know? I will tell you all, show you everything, give you anything."

Her eyes narrowed. "Why? What is in this for you? What do you want from me?"

I shrugged. "In two hundred years, I've not found another soul like yours. I've not found another to rival your spirit, mind, or beauty. I would have you as my partner, as my lover, as my equal."

She slid her hand around to grip my hair in her other hand and pulled me to her. My lips met hers in a soft caress of silk and fire. She was the first drink of water after days in the desert, the first bite of a decadent cake after months of only mush, the first sip of sweet muscadine wine after years of nothing, a breath of fresh air after nearly suffocating, the first glorious touch of warmth after sleeping in the cold for days, and none of those things because she was better than all of those things together.

I lost myself in her touch, in her taste, in her smell, in her. She could have killed me in that moment, and I'd have died happily. To have her kiss me again, I would hold the knife for her. She shifted against me, pressed herself to me, and I nearly lost my mind. I slid my fingers around to the back of her neck, cupped her head in my hand, and deepened the kiss. She sighed against me, and we finally parted.

"Mo shiorghra[1]," I choked out hoarsely. "If you mean to turn me away, it would be kinder to kill me."

Her face was shadowed, her eyes hooded with dark lashes, and her voice barely a whisper.

"You are a very persuasive man. I would sooner destroy a priceless artifact than you."

I held my breath. We'd both forgotten about my arm, mid-suture until I tried to move it, and the pain of the wound came back full force. I was also bleeding again.

"Tell me about yourself while I finish sewing up your arm. I would know more about the man I seem intent upon lashing myself to for the remainder of his days."

My breath left me in a whoosh. I pressed another kiss to her lush mouth, albeit a much quicker one, and my heart soared. Her answering smile was further balm to my weary and terrified soul.

"Where shall I start, mo shiorghra?"

She picked up the needle and began to close the gaping hole in my arm while her beautiful smile filled the empty spaces within my heart I hadn't even known were there.

"Why don't you start by telling me what that means."

I grinned at her, and her breath caught as she bit her lip. I delighted in the response.

"It means my eternal love."

Her answering smile was beatific. I no longer cared what might come next, as long as she and I would be together. As long as we did whatever it was together.

How long is the right amount of time to know you are in love with someone? A week, a month, a year...an hour?

For me, it was mere seconds.

Fairy Tales Or Faery Tails

Prequel

"Dragons were not always here, my girl," Granda said sagely.

I giggled as The Drake nuzzled my neck with his many whiskered face. His large, dark head was almost as big as my four year-old body, and one eye was the size of my head. He ruffled my hair with a snort, and I blinked fast.

My chin wobbled a little when I thought about the way I looked. My hair was shiny silver and red. Not the bright red like Granda's but a mixture of his red and Babushka's black. My eyes weren't even matching right now. One was hazel, and the other was mostly silver. My skin was blotchy, blue in some places, but still peach in others.

One girl at school said I looked like I had a disease. She poked my tummy and told me it was fat, too. I poked my belly, but it was just hungry. The smell of the chicken cooking over the fire was making it grumble loud.

"But Granda, Drake is right here," I said, tickling under Drake's chin with my fingers. He purred.

"Aye, a stoirin, but once he was not. Once dragons were only thoughts in an angry god's head," he said, turning the spit with the chicken on it.

I sighed contentedly. "Are you going to tell me? Which god thunk him?"

"Thought of him," Babushka corrected. She came over to brush my hair and braid it. Mother had left it wild. "We're going to get this hair under control, my darling." She pressed a kiss to my cheek and squeezed me in her arms before going back to the hair. "It's important to manage the image others see. It's fine to be free and wild, but we must always determine the version of us they get to see."

"Yes, Babushka," I said quietly, looking down at my dirty hands.

She pulled my face around to look at her. I stared into her dark blue eyes that shone in the firelight. "You've done nothing wrong, zvezdochka moya," she said firmly, gently shaking my cheek. "You are learning and will be the greatest of us."

Granda made a noise, and I looked at him. He was shaking his head, and his eyes glistened in the light. Babushka said words to him I didn't understand, but he did. He clucked his tongue, and Drake roared out a laugh.

"Be careful, ya great lizard, before you burn this ancient forest down around us. S'been a dry year."

Drake quieted and curled around us. Babushka went back to my hair, but once she was finished brushing and chanting, she handed me over to Granda. He set to braiding my hair. And as he braided, he began his story.

"The gods were jealous of the Fae," he began.

"Why?" I asked.

"Mmm," he said, a smile in his voice. "Why is anyone jealous, Kable?"

I bit my lip and took the blueberries Babushka handed me for a snack. "Because they want your stuff?" I asked, popping a few in my mouth.

He finished one braid and tied it off before moving to the next section. "Well, yes, but it's more than that. Jealousy is wanting something that isn't yours but also about power. For every mean, hurtful, or desperate thing someone does, there is a desire to control, a desire for power." He finished another braid and moved on.

"Not too real, Fynbar, there is time. We must go slowly," Babushka said from the other side of the flames. She'd put corn inside foil into the fire earlier and turned it with her bare hands. I watched in awe as the fire moved around them without burning her. Granda made a sound, and she winked at us.

Drake snored loudly, and I giggled. Granda tickled my side before starting on the section of hair he'd gotten ready.

"Where was I? Oh yes, jealously. The gods were jealous of the Fae because they are not governed by the laws of man the way the gods are."

I frowned. "But they're gods. They don't got rules." Babushka made an *eh* noise, and I sighed. "They don't have rules."

"Everyone has rules, child," he said. "The only difference is who's enforcing them."

That thought made me screw up my face in thought. "But you don't have rules. You're the boss," I finally said.

He laughed, a booming, happy sound that made my lips curl upward. Babushka's eyes twinkled, and I snickered. She'd be kissing him real soon.

"Even I have rules," he said, the laugh tumbling out with his words. He'd started on another braid. They were tingling and warm as he finished with them. Granda always put protections in his braids.

"And a boss, too," Drake said, half-asleep.

Babushka tossed something I couldn't see at Drake, and it bounced off his side to fly into the air behind him. "You two are impossible," she said.

"I did nothing," Granda said. "So, yes, Kable, we all have rules. The rules of gods are convoluted and messy."

I scowled. "What's convoluted?"

"Mmm," he hummed out. "It's a puzzle or a maze."

"Okay," I said. "How many braids, Granda?"

"Enough," he said simply, but I could still hear the smile. "Do you still want to hear about the dragons?"

"Yes, sir," I said, moving my butt to get more comfortable to listen.

"The gods decided to play a game," he started again. His voice was lilting and warm. "They invited the Fae to participate, and they decided on a day."

Drake let out a long snore, and I giggled. Granda was working on another braid, and I heard him speaking words under his breath. He could do spells like that while he talked and did other things. He was the smartest man I knew.

"They gathered on the tournament day with agreed-upon games and rules. But the gods changed the games, and the Fae changed the rules." He smoothed the braids he'd finished and continued. "The games they chose were heavily geared toward the gods. The Fae adjusted the rules, creating three possible avenues for each competition."

"Four," Babushka said, starting a kettle of tea.

"A yes, love," he said. "Thank you. The four possible outcomes were loss, draw, and win. For a loss, they chose to send them to the Crescent Court. For a draw, the Winter Court, and for a win, the Summer Court."

"That's just three," I pointed out.

"Right you are," he said. "Thank you for keeping the count. The last for cheaters, and they sent them to the UpAbove."

"The UpAbove?" I asked. "With the angels, Granda?"

"Yes, with those Devils," he said, his voice gruff.

"No, Granda, you said Angels," I admonished.

"That I did, love. You must know that just because something is lovely on the outside doesn't make it lovely on the inside," he said quietly as his fingers moved through my hair. He was nearly done.

"What like a poisonous flower? Or a pretty spider?" I asked.

"Exactly, zvezdochka," Babushka said. "The lovelier something is, the more you must be wary."

I scowled. "But you're beautiful, and you're good. So's Granda. And my babies are the prettiest, and they are NOT bad," I said matter-of-factly.

She smiled across the fire, and her eyes glowed blue. Her hair was wild and swirling in the breeze. "You're right, of course. There are many beautiful things that are also good. But, darling girl, not all of them are. Angels are only as good as their hearts. They only have a soul if they're fallen."

She took a breath, and the smoke from the fire circled around her. The starlight gathered in her eyes, and Granda's hands stopped moving. She twisted her hands, and the fire breathed before it flared bright, throwing sparks. She sang into the night and danced with her shawls. The fire danced with her for two whole songs. Granda and I watched, barely breathing. Babushka was so pretty it made my chest hurt, and my eyes cry fat tears. I couldn't keep the happy from spilling out.

She came over to us, and Granda began braiding again. "You will meet an Angel or two, Kable. There will be one who will steal your doubts and give you wings. There will be another who will fan your flame and eat your passion." Her eyes were flames, and her voice was spooky.

"I don't wanna meet a scary angel," I whispered.

She bent forward, kissing my cool cheeks with her warm lips. "You will love one more than life, and the other's existence will tangle the web. They will both affect your life."

"But Babushka, I don't wanna. I'm gonna be a warrior woman with my wolf fighting with me. We're gonna fight monsters," I told her. My face was screwed up in my battle face, and I jabbed out like I was stabbing with a sword. I didn't really have a sword; it was just a stick.

"Fynbar, finish your tale," she said, standing back with arms crossed over her chest and a slight smile on her lips.

He grunted before going on. "Where was I?"

"Scary angels," I said, looking up at the sky.

"Well," he said, chuckling. "I suppose that's where it started." His fingers moved over my hair. The braids were done, and he was adding yarn and beads. "The cheaters went to the UpAbove to pay penance."

"But why didn't they go Underneath?" I couldn't help asking. "Isn't the Underneath for bad people?"

"No," Granda said, snorting. "They are none of them good or bad. They simply are. Each of them is a construct, existing because we believe they should. Our belief makes them real."

I pulled my head forward and then turned to look at him. "Huh? Like, I believe there's chocolate cake, so there's cake?" I asked.

Babushka laughed long and hard before handing me a slice of chocolate cake. My eyes were round, but I settled back to let Granda finish and ate my cake.

"So now that your little mouth is full and can't ask so many questions," he teased, "perhaps I can finish this tale." I giggled, and his voice was smiling. "The cheaters went to the UpAbove, where they were given jobs to do. But cheaters, being cheaters, did what they always do."

I nodded sagely, licking the icing off my spoon. "They cheated."

"Yes," he said. "And they were caught by the Angels. Michael was so angry at their deception that he wanted to smite them, but Raphael felt sorry for them. He convinced Michael to give them another chance. They sent them to Eden to tend the garden."

"Oooh," I said, licking the chocolate icing off my finger.

"Yes," he said, continuing to weave.

Babushka watched us with a soft smile while she trailed her fingers over Drake's tale. He purred so loud it tickled inside my chest. I grinned so wide it made my face hurt a little.

"They worked hard and eventually were allowed to explore Eden," he continued. "When they explored an underwater cave, they found a nest with beautiful, jeweled eggs." I listened hard, trying not to miss anything. "They were submerged in the deep cave, frozen." He paused, took a deep breath, and blew frosty, foggy air over me. I shivered and giggled. He tickled me before continuing.

"They brought the eggs up and showed them to Ezekiel. He took them before Raphael, who gifted them to the finders for outstanding work. He told them to warm the eggs in a full moon bonfire and wait."

I looked at our bonfire under the fat moon and then at Babushka. She smiled at my cleverness and nodded.

"The six that found the eggs took them, built the largest bonfire they could, and awaited the night and the moon." His hands had stopped moving in my hair, and I moved to sit with my back to Drake to see Granda and Babushka. "They put in thirteen eggs and sang beautiful songs of love and bond throughout the night. When the fire finally burned down seven days later, twelve little winged lizards walked out, breathing fire and growling."

My breath caught. "Where did they come from? Where was their momma?"

"No one knows," Granda said softly.

Drake's breathing changed behind me, and his head came around on his long neck to look at me and the fire. "An old question, that," he said. "Dragon or egg, which came first?" He snorted. "We never found a trace of a mother, only the cave and the eggs."

I scratched under his chin. "You were one of the babies, Drake? I bet you were sooo cute," I cooed.

Granda snorted then. "He's always been a pain in my backside. Big, little, old, or young." His voice was stern, but his face was laughing.

"Why do we put up with him, Katya?" Drake asked Babushka. He was the only one who called her Katya.

"We love the old fool to a distraction," she replied.

"Ah yes," Drake rumbled. "How is our own jeweled treasure doing?" he asked.

She frowned. "No change. Perhaps we must freeze it first?"

"Do you know a way into Eden?" he asked.

She grimaced. "None I'd like to test."

My eyes moved between them all as they spoke. I was playing with the beads in my hair. They made my fingers tingle as I touched them lightly.

"What say you, Fynbar? Do we wait the seven days or try freezing?" Drake asked.

Granda stroked his beard thoughtfully. Drake started to speak again, but Granda held up a hand as his eyes drifted around our campsite. He wasn't looking at anything here.

I sat back with my hands cupping my chin to watch. Granda was the cleverest when he was like that. He'd sit like that and suddenly jump up to drag me with him to create. We'd made special bracelets for the Werewolves last time. And when we'd taken them to their leader, he'd shown me their nursery with the babies. I'd met a boy who was older than me with light brown eyes, teak-colored skin, and dark brown hair. He'd shown me where they kept the bad wolves. His name was Toinne.

"Take it out of the fire," Granda finally said.

Drake reached into the fire and pulled a beautiful football-sized egg out. It was all the colors of the rainbow and shiny like jewels.

"What have you thought of?" Drake asked.

"It is not that the cave in Eden was special; it was the cold. We must incubate the egg in the frozen depths before maturing it in the fires." He looked at the egg. "We will have to wait to see if we've damaged it in any way."

Drake harrumphed. "It will be the first of our kind since my litter. We cannot do worse than all before us. We've lost nothing but time if it does not work."

"Can I touch it?" I breathed out.

They all looked around at me as if they'd forgotten I was there. Drake turned to place the egg in my lap. It was warm but not hot. I lifted it into my arms, cradling it like a baby. Baby Karmine wouldn't let me snuggle her like that anymore, but the egg seemed happy. I sang to it and rocked the rainbow baby inside until my arms were too sore to hold it up. Then, I laid down with it cuddled next to me in my blankets with my back still pressed to Drake.

I snuggled them while they talked about where they would take the egg and ate dinner. I petted them and told them how beautiful they were. I told them a story about Drake so they'd know his bravery. I told them how I loved them and we would always be friends. And finally, I told them how fantastic they were going to be. I told them how I loved them, and we would always be friends. And finally, I told them how fantastic they were going to be.

Babushka came over to get me to eat, but I wasn't hungry. She *tsked* but let me stay with the egg. Granda and Drake murmured, their voices lulling me. I pulled the egg closer and let my eyes drift to Babushka. She poked the fire, and sparkling ashes rose to the heavens. Her dark hair floated around her in the night breeze. She looked up and then back down at me with benevolent eyes.

"And my sweet girl, as for either being a Warrior Woman with your wolf or meeting scary Angels to tame or test, you will do both and more."

A smile crept over my lips, and I fell asleep knowing I was blessed, loved, and safe.

More Titles by MJ Hutto

~In the KableVerse~
Choosing Chaos Series
Kable VonSable

Masquerade in Chaos (1)

Chasing Chaos (2)
Shadows of Chaos (3)
Drowning in Chaos (4)
Chaos Liaison Series
Anastasia Eos
Chaos Dancing (1)

TO FIND OUT MORE ABOUT MJ Hutto, available titles, links, and more: https://www.thekableverse.com[1]https://www.patreon.com/mjhutto_Kableverse

---

[1] "Mo shíorghrá" (muh HEER-ggrawh)

---

1. https://www.thekableverse.com/

Don't miss out!

Visit the website below and you can sign up to receive emails whenever MJ Hutto publishes a new book. There's no charge and no obligation.

https://books2read.com/r/B-A-XCSMD-JOFCG

BOOKS 2 READ

Connecting independent readers to independent writers.

www.ingramcontent.com/pod-product-compliance
Lightning Source LLC
Chambersburg PA
CBHW021133130726
47988CB00003B/1287